Special in Their Own Way

Not Everyone Can Fly Upside Down

Dr. Tiffany Vickers

Illustrations by Blueberry Illustrations

ISBN: 979-8-9859036-0-7

This book is dedicated to every child.

Remember, you are special in your own way.

In the forest, there lived a hummingbird named Lea. She was small and full of beautiful colors. She loved to flit around the forest, saying hi to all her friends.

In fact, she loved flying so much that she had become an expert flyer.

Her wings would beat so fast that she could even fly backwards and upside down! Moving in loops, she felt happy and free flying through the forest.

All of the other birds were so impressed with Lea that she decided to teach them everything she knew about flying.

One day, they all gathered at the edge of the forest.

Lea gave a great performance—loop-the-loops, zipping and zapping, and hovering perfectly still in the air.

They tried their best to copy her but ...

it did not go well. No one could do what Lea could do.

This made Lea very sad. She loved how it felt to fly backwards and upside down and wanted everyone else to try it for themselves.

"Don't be sad!" said Angela the Penguin. "I might not be able to fly, but I can swim instead!"

Angela plunged into the water to show everyone what she could do.

"My wings are called flippers and they let me dive deeper into the ocean than any other bird! I can even hold my breath for nearly 20 minutes!"

Everyone was very impressed with Angela, but Lea still looked sad.

"What about the others?" asked Lea. "They can't swim or fly upside down." Maricella the Flamingo smiled. "I might not be able to fly upside down, but I can eat upside down!"

Maricella dunked her beak into the water to show everyone what she could do. "My special beak lets me catch lots of tasty food. In fact, eating lots of shrimp is why I'm so beautifully pink! I can also stand on one leg so that my other leg can have a rest!"

Everyone was very impressed with Maricella, but Lea still looked sad.

"No one is as beautifully pink as you, Maricella," said Lea, "and they can't swim like Angela or fly like me."

Anderson the Peacock strutted forward. "I might not be pink but I am most certainly beautiful!"

Anderson spread out his tail feathers in a glorious display of glittering green and blue.

"My tail is so beautiful that everyone can't help but look at me!" he said.

Everyone was very impressed with Anderson, but Lea still looked sad.

William the Ostrich smiled. "Are you sad that I can't do all of these things?" he asked.

"I can't swim or fly and I don't have a special beak or beautiful tail feathers, but I do have the strongest legs of any bird and no one else can run as fast as I can!"

William raced around them all so fast that they all got rather dizzy.

When Lea saw all of the impressive things that the others could do, she realized she wasn't sad anymore.

"Of course! We're all experts at different things and that's what makes us each special in our own way."

About the Author

TIFFANY VICKERS, DNP, RN is a writer and holder of multiple degrees in nursing. She uses her experience and passion to create inspiring stories for young children. With her children's book *Special in Their Own Way*, she brings together all of her talents in an inspiring tale of what it really means to be special.

A native of Florida, Dr. Tiffany developed an early love for animals and learned the value of educating oneself about the world. She hopes to use her stories to encourage young children to be proud of their accomplishments and to pursue their own success in the world.

CPSIA information can be obtained
at www.ICGtesting.com
Printed in the USA
BVHW020946080622
639211BV00007B/238